Pro Football
Hall of Fame

by
Terry Janson Dunnahoo
and
Herma Silverstein

Crestwood House
New York

Maxwell Macmillan Canada
Toronto

Maxwell Macmillan International
New York   Oxford   Singapore   Sydney

Dedication
To my grandnephew Jason
TJD
To my Uncle R, football fan and special consultant
HS

Library of Congress Cataloging-in-Publication Data
Dunnahoo, Terry.
Pro Football Hall of Fame / by Terry Janson Dunnahoo and Herma Silverstein. — 1st ed.
p. cm. — (The Halls of fame)
Includes index.
Summary: Presents a history of football and details about the Pro Football Hall of Fame, including its exhibits, famous members, and rules of selection.
ISBN 0-89686-851-6
1. Pro Football Hall of Fame (U. S.) — Juvenile literature.
2. Football — United States — History — Juvenile literature. [1. Pro Football Hall of Fame (U. S.)
2. Football — History.]
I. Silverstein, Herma. II. Title. III. Series.
GV959.5.U6D86 1994   796.332'0973 — dc20   93-954

Photo Credits
Photo on page 18 courtesy of AP/Wide World Photos
All other photos courtesy of the Pro Football Hall of Fame, Canton, Ohio
The publishers have made every effort to locate the copyright holders, but if they have overlooked any, they will be pleased to make the necessary arrangements at the first opportunity.

Design
Tina Tarr Emmons

Layout and Production
Custom Communications

Crestwood House
Macmillan Publishing Company
866 Third Avenue
New York, NY 10022

Maxwell Macmillan Canada, Inc.
1200 Eglinton Avenue East
Suite 200
Don Mills, Ontario M3C 3N1

Macmillan Publishing Company is part of the Maxwell Communication Group of Companies.
First Edition
Printed in the United States of America
10 9 8 7 6 5 4 3 2 1

Table of Contents

A display at the Pro Football Hall of Fame shows the early history of football. Inset: William W. (Pudge) Heffelfinger, a Yale University All-American guard, was the first known athlete to receive payment for playing in a football game.

Chapter One

The Game Plan: The Birth of Football

How would you like to **scrimmage** against quarterback Fran Tarkenton, running back O. J. Simpson, or the all-time great, halfback Jim Thorpe?

You can. Just visit the Pro Football Hall of Fame in Canton, Ohio. Through its displays of famous players, coaches, and games, the Hall of Fame, opened in 1963, traces the history of pro football back to its beginnings in 1892.

The game of football probably owes its origin to a temper tantrum thrown by British soccer player William Webb Ellis. During a soccer game at Rugby School in England in 1823, Ellis was having an off day. Every time he tried to kick the ball, he missed. So he picked it up and ran. But carrying the ball was against the rules.

Other players thought carrying the ball made the game more fun and copied Ellis. Some soccer coaches didn't agree, but other coaches liked the idea. So in 1841 those coaches made up a new sport called rugby football. The game allowed players to kick and carry the ball. And from **rugby** came football.

There is evidence that a primitive type of football was played in the 13 colonies at least as early as 1700. But football as we know it didn't get off the ground until Europeans settled in America and brought soccer and rugby with them. The game of rugby football was snapped up by universities in the northeastern United States, especially Princeton, Rutgers, Columbia, Yale, and Harvard. There were 15 men on each team. In 1867 the first official rules were set down, called the Princeton Rules. Two years later, on November 6, the first game between colleges was played, in New Brunswick, New Jersey. Rutgers beat Princeton, 6-4.

Early American football stayed a kicking game more than a running game, although Harvard liked to run with the ball more than kick it. So in 1874 Harvard invited a rugby team from McGill University in Montreal, Canada, to come to Cambridge, Massachusetts, and play against Harvard.

When the McGill team arrived on May 15, 4 of their 15 players got sick. The game had to be played with 11 players on each side. If the 4 players from McGill hadn't become ill, today's football might still be played with 15 players.

On November 13, 1875, Harvard played Yale with the 11-man team. A year later, on November 23, in Springfield, Massachusetts, players from Princeton, Rutgers, Columbia, Yale, and Harvard drew up rules based on rugby. These players called themselves the Intercollegiate Football Association.

College football really caught on. The games were played in big cities. Small cities like Greensburg and Latrobe, Pennsylvania, which weren't near colleges, wanted to get in on the football action, too. So they formed football teams sponsored by athletic clubs to play in their towns.

To get the best amateur players, some clubs gave them expensive trophies or watches. The players pawned these "rewards" to get money. Then the owners bought the pawned rewards and gave them back to the players. The Amateur Athletic Union (AAU), an organization which was founded in 1888 to supervise and conduct amateur athletic developmental programs and competition, did not like this process of recycling rewards. But every time the AAU stopped the recycling, athletic clubs found other ways to "pay" players.

The payoffs worked. So many fans loved these football games that by the 1890s most athletic clubs had semipro football teams playing for them.

In 1892 something happened that ignited the beginning of pro football. The Allegheny Athletic Association was competing with the Pittsburgh

Athletic Club to get William W. "Pudge" Heffelfinger, a Yale University All-American guard, to play on its team. The battle raged until finally, on November 12, the Allegheny association decided to win the war for Heffelfinger by paying him $500 to play one game against the Pittsburgh club.

Heffelfinger was worth the $500. He won the game by tackling the opposing halfback. The ball jarred loose and Heffelfinger grabbed the **fumble**, then raced across the goal line for the only score of the game. At the time, a **touchdown** was worth 4 points, so the score was 4-0, Allegheny.

Pittsburgh protested the payoff but couldn't prove the illegal action. It wasn't until 80 years later, when someone sent an expense account sheet of the Allegheny Athletic Association to the Pro Football Hall of Fame, that proof of a payoff was found. On the accounting sheet were the words "Game performance to W. Heffelfinger for playing (cash) $500." Heffelfinger was the first documented pro football player in the world.

The paying of money instead of trophies and watches to a football player was the beginning of football's big time — pro football.

Football hero Jim Thorpe is featured in a display at the Pro Football Hall of Fame. Inset: *Thorpe was a Native American who served as president of the first major league football organization.*

Chapter Two

Backfield in Motion: The Gridiron Goes Pro

With today's pro football games televised all around the world and million-dollar salaries paid to players, it's hard to believe that big-time pro football began in a car dealership showroom in Canton, Ohio.

On August 20, 1920, representatives from four athletic clubs met at the Jordan and Hupmobile Auto Showroom in Canton. At that meeting, the American Professional Football Conference (APFC) was formed. More clubs wanted to join. So on September 17 another meeting was held in Canton. And yet another organization was born — the American Professional Football Association (APFA). This was football's first major league. And Jim Thorpe, halfback for the Canton Bulldogs, was elected president.

Thorpe, whose Native American name was Wa-Tho-Huck, meaning Bright Path, was an all-around athlete. Thorpe was tops in baseball, lacrosse, and high jumping at the Carlisle Institute in Pennsylvania. But he was kept on the bench during football games. And he probably would never have played football if Carlisle's halfback hadn't gotten hurt in a 1907 game. Thorpe was sent in as a substitute. His 65- and 85-yard touchdowns helped the Carlisle team beat top-ranked Penn State. He later went on to win two gold medals at the 1912 Olympics.

For these athletic accomplishments and for his pro football accomplishments, which began in 1915, Thorpe was chosen as president of the APFA.

The APFA struggled through its first season, in 1920. Most teams played from 7 to 11 games. A couple of them played 13 games, and one team played only 1 game. At the end of the first season, not only did the teams need to have a regular game schedule, but the APFA's rules also had to be revised to make football better organized. Helmets and other protective equipment practically didn't exist. And teams bulldozed each other to the ground.

One of the men who helped draw up the 1921 rule changes was the APFA's new president, Joe Carr, a sportswriter and **promoter** who had founded the Columbus Panhandles team in 1904.

Carr held the job of APFA president until his death in 1939. With fairness and efficiency in his strict enforcement of the rules, Carr improved the APFA's reputation. In 1922 the APFA was renamed the National Football League (NFL).

Through Carr's introduction of the standard players' contract, the NFL tried to limit the team salary to $1,200 per game per team, including the coach. But no one went along with this salary limit. Today pro football players make more money than the president of the United States, some earning over $1 million a year.

Joe Carr, a sportswriter and promoter, served as president of the APFA and tried to limit the salary for each football team to $1,200 per game.

Chapter Three

The NFL Grows Up and the AFL Is Born

As part of his revision of football rules, Joe Carr barred the NFL from hiring college students before their class graduated. Any pro team that tried to recruit a college player before his class graduated would be fined $1,000. This rule was written because of George Halas, owner of the Chicago Bears. Halas signed All-American halfback Harold "Red" Grange right after his final game for the University of Illinois in November 1925 — before he graduated.

That same month Grange played his first pro game for the Bears on Thanksgiving Day against the Chicago Cardinals. He was known as the Galloping Ghost because he could break through the best defenses. Grange would come to a dead stop, then whirl in another direction and take off down the field, leaving his tacklers in the dust. Because of his talent and the business smarts of his agent, Charles C. Pyle, Grange got thousands of dollars for playing eight games in 12 days.

After the pro season ended, the Bears traveled around the country on two **barnstorming tours**. People mobbed the stadiums to see Grange play. He made almost $100,000 that season. The New York game alone on that tour earned him $30,000. No player had ever pocketed that much money in a season, and none would for many years.

Grange's agent, Pyle, asked Bears' owner Halas for one-third owner-

A uniform worn by early football players is displayed at the Pro Football Hall of Fame. Inset: Harold "Red" Grange, known as the Galloping Ghost, earned more than any other player of his time.

ship of the team. Halas refused, so Pyle tried to get an NFL franchise. When the NFL refused, Pyle put together a new league in 1926 called the American Football League (AFL). The league had nine teams and lasted only one season. So Grange went back to the NFL. After playing for one season with the NFL's New York Yankees and sitting out another, Grange returned to the Bears in 1929.

During the 1930s the NFL was making great headway and major changes. One of the most important came in 1933. For the first time the NFL developed its own rule book. Until then the NFL had been using the college rule book and had made only small changes to those rules. One of the reasons for the new rules was to create a more exciting offensive game.

The year 1933 also marked the first NFL Championship game. At that time, the ten teams of the NFL were divided into the Eastern and Western divisions. The season ended with the first official NFL Championship game. The Chicago Bears beat the New York Giants, 23-21.

Star NFL players like Jim Thorpe, Ernie Nevers, Joe Guyon, and Paddy Driscoll were replaced by newcomers Clarke Hinkle, Mel Hein, Johnny "Blood" McNally, and Bronko Nagurski. Hinkle, who played with the Green Bay Packers from 1932 to 1941, was multitalented. He played fullback and linebacker. And he did everything on the field well — ran, passed, placekicked, **punted**, and caught passes. He and Nagurski had many head-on clashes on the field when the Packers played the Bears.

Nagurski, who joined the Chicago Bears in 1930, was pro football's symbol of power and ruggedness because of his bulldozing offensive running and bone-crushing linebacking. He was voted All-NFL for three years straight — 1932, 1933, and 1934. In 1937 he retired, only to come back six years later and help the Bears win the NFL crown in 1943.

During the 1930s some significant firsts occurred in the NFL. The first college **draft** was held in 1936. In 1939 the first broadcast of an NFL game — the Philadelphia Eagles against the Brooklyn Dodgers, from Ebbets Field, on NBC   was aired on the radio. And the total league attendance was over a million for the first time.

Football became a passing game instead of a running game, mainly because of the plays of Don Hutson. Hutson played for the Green Bay Packers from 1935 to 1945. He was the NFL's first "super end" and in

This Hall of Fame exhibit illustrates how the rules governing pro football have changed through the years and lists the rules in effect today.

1969 was named the NFL's all-time end.

In the 1940s football started and ended with a bang. The Chicago Bears won the 1940 championship with an incredible 73-0 victory over the Washington Redskins. Then, at the close of the decade, in 1948, the Philadelphia Eagles beat the Chicago Cardinals, 7-0, in the title game, and in 1949 the Eagles won the championship by defeating the Los Angeles Rams, 14-0. The Eagles became the only team to post two straight championship game shutouts in NFL history.

With the success of the NFL, other teams got together to try to form rival leagues. Although neither of the two new leagues had any connection to the earlier AFL, they were named the American Football League. One was formed in 1936-1937 and the other in 1940-1941. Both failed.

Another effort to compete with the NFL was made in 1946, with the creation of the short-lived All-America Football Conference (AAFC). This league had eight teams, including the Cleveland Browns, who were the best in the league, with a four-year record of 52-4-3. The AAFC lasted four years and broke up after the 1949 season. In 1950 Cleveland, the Baltimore Colts, and the San Francisco 49ers joined the NFL. The Browns had a 10-2 record and won the NFL title with a 30-28 win over the Los Angeles Rams in the 1950 NFL Championship game.

In 1959 the first attempt to create a rival league to the NFL since the AAFC occurred. Dallas millionaire Lamar Hunt was refused an NFL franchise, so he created a new American Football League (AFL). The first games were played in 1960 with eight teams. Another millionaire, David A. "Sonny" Werblin, gave the AFL a boost in 1963 when he bought the struggling New York Titans and changed the team's name to the Jets. Two years later the Jets drafted Alabama super quarterback Joe Namath. Signing Namath was a smart move for the AFL and the kickoff for the merger of the NFL and AFL into one organization, the National Football League (NFL).

During the years before the merger, the NFL grew stronger under football commissioner Pete Rozelle. Rozelle, former manager of the Los Angeles Rams, was commissioner for almost 30 years and the most respected and admired commissioner in all of sports. Football fans can thank Rozelle for their favorite day of every year — **Super Bowl** Sunday.

Pete Rozelle, inducted into the Pro Football Hall of Fame in 1985, came up with the idea of holding a Super Bowl championship game every year.

Joe Namath, star quarterback for the New York Jets, gets ready to throw a pass during the 1969 Super Bowl game with the Baltimore Colts.

Chapter Four

The Super Bowl: Super Games, Super Plays, Super Players

Before there was a Super Bowl, there was a championship NFL game at the end of the regular football season, called the National Football League Championship. The first was in 1933, when the Chicago Bears beat the New York Giants, 23-21. The winners got $210.34 each, the losers $140.22 each.

In the mid-1960s the bidding battle between the NFL and the AFL exploded into outright war — a conflict that would lead to the Super Bowl. In 1965, when Joe Namath signed with the AFL's Jets, he received about $400,000. This was the most money ever paid to a college player. The following year, to stay in the competition, the NFL's Atlanta Falcons paid Texas linebacker Tommy Nobis $600,000, and the Green Bay Packers forked over $711,000 to Texas Tech running back Donny Anderson.

Meanwhile, the salaries of seasoned pro players didn't come close to the **rookies**' salaries. NFL quarterback John Brodie of the San Francisco 49ers was getting $35,000 in 1965. And this was after he led the NFL in completions, yardage, and touchdown passes.

On April 8, 1966, Hall of Famer Al Davis, owner and general manager of the Oakland Raiders — later renamed the Los Angeles Raiders — became AFL commissioner. He told AFL owners to pay NFL quarterbacks big money to switch to the AFL. Almost immediately the AFL signed NFL

Bart Starr, quarterback for the Green Bay Packers, was voted Most Valuable Player in the first and second Super Bowl games.

stars to future contracts that would be effective as soon as their NFL contracts were up. More than a dozen players, including several big-name NFL quarterbacks, were rumored to be thinking about joining the AFL.

With the prospect of losing its quarterbacks, the NFL was backed into a corner. On June 8, 1966, a settlement and a merger agreement were reached.

There would be a common draft starting in 1967. And the two leagues agreed to have a yearly championship game against each other. The game would be called the AFL-NFL World Championship — later renamed the Super Bowl. The first championship game would be played on January 15, 1967.

Another part of the agreement said that starting in 1970, the NFL and AFL would be divided into the National Football Conference (NFC) and the American Football Conference (AFC). The two conferences would make up one league, called the National Football League (NFL).

The first championship game was announced in December 1966. That gave fans only a month to buy tickets. So even though the tickets sold for $8, $10, and $12, only 61,946 fans showed up. The first game was played at Memorial Coliseum in Los Angeles. Vince Lombardi's Green Bay Packers trounced the Kansas City Chiefs, 35-10.

Before the teams agreed to play, compromises had to be made. A Wilson football had to be used when the NFL was on offense. A Spalding ball had to be used when the AFL was on offense. Even the television networks were at war. CBS, known as the NFL network, and NBC, known as the AFL network, wanted to broadcast the game. Neither would give in. So each network paid $1 million to televise the championship.

Packers quarterback Bart Starr was voted Most Valuable Player, after completing 16 of 23 passes. In 1968 he did an instant MVP replay when the Packers beat the Oakland Raiders, 33-14, in the second AFL-NFL World Championship game. Hard to believe, but this two-time MVP wasn't picked for a pro team until the seventeenth round in the 1956 football draft. Starr went on to lead the Packers to five NFL titles. In his career he threw 152 touchdowns and passed for a total of 24,718 yards.

Besides talent, Starr had another plus going for him. That was Green Bay Packers coach Lombardi. Some people consider Lombardi the greatest

Displayed along a wall of the Hall of Fame are helmets of all the teams in the American and National Football conferences. Inset: Lamar Hunt, Dallas millionaire who created a new American Football League, named the championship game the Super Bowl.

coach who ever lived. He provided his team members with a will to win, not only on the football field but in life as well. In fact, many of Lombardi's players have gone on to lead very successful lives after retiring from pro football.

After the Packers won the second AFL-NFL World Championship, Lombardi said he was retiring. But he couldn't stay away from football. It was his life. In the spring of 1969, Lombardi became head coach and executive vice president of the Washington Redskins. His stay with the

Redskins was cut short, though. Lombardi died of cancer on September 3, 1970. In his honor, the Super Bowl Trophy was renamed the Lombardi Trophy.

It wasn't until the third AFL-NFL World Championship that the game was renamed the Super Bowl and the words were printed on tickets and game programs. NFL officials had resisted the name Super Bowl because they thought it was undignified. The name change got its kickoff during the preseason, when Kansas City Chiefs' owner Lamar Hunt asked if the teams should be given one or two weeks to get ready for the "championship game."

Someone asked him, "Which championship game? The AFL or the NFL?" Hunt said, "I mean the last game, the final game, you know, the *super bowl*." Hunt came up with the idea after seeing his daughter Sharon's toy called a Super Ball. "If you threw one down hard on the concrete," he said, "it would literally bounce over the house."

Later Pete Rozelle added, "With the press calling the game Super Bowl and Hunt repeating the name, fans wouldn't let the game be called anything else."

Credit for the Roman numerals tied to each game goes to Hunt, too. While reading the paper after the third Super Bowl, he saw a headline: JETS ARE TERRIFIC IN SUPER III. He thought the Roman numerals looked classy, so he cut out the article and mailed it to Rozelle with a note: "Here's a way to classy up our not so classy name." The next game was billed as Super Bowl IV.

Super Bowl V brought another superstar coach to the game when Tom Landry coached his Dallas Cowboys in a close loss to the Baltimore Colts, 16-13. Head coach of the Cowboys for 29 years, Landry turned the Cowboys from a winless franchise into one that became known as America's Team, posting 20 straight winning seasons.

In the 1970s the Cowboys went to the Super Bowl five times and won twice. Then in the mid-1980s the Cowboys began to slide. In 1988 the team finished with a 3-13 record. So in February 1989 Jerry Jones, an oil millionaire from Little Rock, Arkansas, bought the Cowboys. He fired Landry and hired his college buddy Jimmy Johnson, former coach at Oklahoma State and Miami.

Getting rid of Landry set off fireworks. Texans were up in arms. They marched in the streets and pelted Jones's pictures with trash, as if he'd torched the Alamo. When the Cowboys won only 1 game out of 16 during Johnson's first season, the protests grew wilder. Johnson didn't pay attention to all the name-calling. Instead he promised that the Cowboys would be in a Super Bowl within five years. They made it in four. In Super Bowl XXVII, played in January 1993, the Cowboys beat the Buffalo Bills, 52-17.

In his first draft choice as the Cowboys' coach, Johnson picked UCLA quarterback Troy Aikman. Aikman threw four touchdown passes in Super Bowl XXVII. It was his first Super Bowl game, and he was voted MVP. When someone asked Aikman whether he thought he deserved the MVP Award, he said, "I'm a little bashful about receiving it."

Super Bowl XXVII was a record-setting game — some bad stats, some good. It marked the ninth AFC Super Bowl loss in a row. The Bills became the first team to lose three consecutive Super Bowls and the team that fumbled the most in any Super Bowl — eight times. The good news went to the Cowboys. They became the team that played in the most Super Bowls — six.

Another remarkable Super Bowl for the Cowboys was Super Bowl XIII, which took place in the 1970s. Played between the Cowboys and the Pittsburgh Steelers, this was a real edge-of-the-seat game. With seven minutes left on the clock, the score was 35-17, Steelers. The Cowboys made a brilliant comeback. Roger Staubach threw two touchdown passes — one to Billy Joe DuPree and the other to Butch Johnson — making the score 35-31.

With only 22 seconds remaining, Steelers quarterback Terry Bradshaw took the snap twice and twice fell on the ball to use up time. The clock ran out and the Steelers won, becoming the first team to win three Super Bowls. Bradshaw was voted MVP.

Players from both teams raved about Bradshaw's passing — 318 yards and four touchdowns. Cowboys safety Charlie Waters, losing like a good sport, said, "He throws a football 20 yards like I throw a dart 15 feet. I'll think a lot about Bradshaw during the off-season. Unfortunately the pain will get worse before it gets better."

Along the hallway leading to the second building of the Pro Football Hall of Fame are bronze busts of all the Hall of Fame members.

And winning like a good sport, Steelers defensive tackle Joe Greene said, "The Cowboys are good enough that on any given Sunday they might beat us."

And on any given Sunday during football season, you might catch a super game that could take your favorite team to the next Super Bowl.

A Hall of Fame exhibit shows how football uniforms have changed through the years. Inset: Steelers defensive tackle "Mean" Joe Greene, who played on the winning team in Super Bowl XIII, was inducted into the Hall in 1987.

The Pro Football Hall of Fame was opened in Canton, Ohio, on September 7, 1963. Inset: Greeting visitors to the Hall of Fame is a statue of Jim Thorpe, who played his first pro games with the Canton Bulldogs.

Chapter Five

Touchdown: Pro Football Builds a Hall of Fame

"PRO FOOTBALL NEEDS A HALL OF FAME AND LOGICAL SITE IS HERE."

These words headlined the *Canton Repository* newspaper on December 6, 1959. Local officials thought their city was the best place for a Pro Football Hall of Fame. One of their reasons was that the American Professional Football Association, which became the NFL, was founded in Canton.

Another reason was that the Canton Bulldogs were one of the top early pro football teams. They were NFL champions in 1922 and 1923. And city officials pointed out that the "greatest athlete of all time," Jim Thorpe, played his first pro games with the Bulldogs in 1915.

In 1961 the NFL agreed to let Canton, Ohio, be the home of the Pro Football Hall of Fame. The people of Canton were so happy to have this honor that the city donated the land, and on September 7, 1963, the first visitors entered the new museum of professional football.

Since then the Hall has collected so much memorabilia that by 1978 it had added two more buildings. When you walk through the door, you'll see ahead of you a 7-foot bronze statue of Jim Thorpe. Walk up the ramp, which curves up around a dome shaped like a football, to the Exhibition Rotunda, where displays show the history of pro football from its beginnings to the birth of the NFL in the 1920s.

Here you'll see the oldest football still in existence, used around 1895.

The photo art gallery features the winning pictures of football games and players from the Hall of Fame's annual contest for professional photographers.

You'll also see a uniform from pro football's first indoor game, held in New York's Madison Square Garden in 1902. Keep looking and you'll see the Thorpe and Canton Bulldogs displays, which include Thorpe's Bulldogs sideline blanket and his 1912 Olympics jacket.

Look at the locker, uniform, and equipment trunk of fullback Ernie Nevers. Nevers played for the Duluth Eskimos in 1926 and 1927. In 1926 the Eskimos played a backbreaking schedule of 29 games, 28 of them on the road.

Special displays show Eric Dickerson's 2,105-yard rushing season in

1984, quarterback Johnny Unitas's feat of throwing at least one touchdown pass in 47 straight games for the Baltimore Colts, and running back Walter Payton's all-time career rushing record of 16,726 yards.

Now enjoy some of the great moments in NFL history as you watch a video of 16 fantastic finishes. Then onward and upward to the Professional Football Today display, where all current NFL teams are honored.

Pass through a hallway leading to the second building, where you will find the first of the twin enshrinement galleries. Here each Hall of Famer is honored with a bronze bust, a mural, and a brief biography.

Also in the second building is an action feature video called *The Kickoff Series* and a photo art gallery. The gallery features the winning photos of football games and players from the Hall of Fame's annual contest for professional photographers.

Between the second and third buildings is the temporary enshrinement area, where the Hall's newest members are honored for one year after their induction. They are then moved to a permanent place in the enshrinement gallery.

In the third building is the second of the twin enshrinement galleries and another video, *Legends of the Game*, which shows interviews with Hall of Famers. And see the Pro Football Adventure Room, with its displays of the Miami Dolphins' perfect 17-0-0 1972 season, the Pro Bowl All-Star Game History, the Evolution of the Uniform, the Teams of the NFL, and the Black Man in Pro Football, including an interview with Fritz Pollard, black player-coach during the 1920s.

Pollard was a star halfback and the first black professional football coach. Among the teams he coached and played for were the Akron Pros, Milwaukee Badgers, and Hammond Pros. Pollard's career was unique at a time when black people weren't given leadership positions. And after Pollard the NFL didn't have another black head coach until Art Shell in 1989.

No blacks played in the NFL from 1933 to 1945. Then in 1946 the Rams signed Kenny Washington and Woody Strode of UCLA. And the Browns of the AAFC signed Marion Motley of Nevada and Bill Willis of Ohio State. The first black player elected to the Hall of Fame was Emlen Tunnell, in 1967. Later both Motley and Willis were also elected to the Hall of Fame.

Today many other black athletes are in the Hall of Fame, including O. J. Simpson, John Mackey, and Charley Taylor.

In the third building you'll see the Byron "Whizzer" White Humanitarian Award. A pro football player, White became a U.S. Supreme Court justice. The Humanitarian Award is given every year by the NFL Players Association to a player for outstanding contributions to society.

As you go into the fourth building, look at the Top Twenty display. It shows lifetime statistics for best passing, rushing, pass receiving, and scoring. During the NFL season, the Top Twenty is changed every week.

And in the Enshrinees Mementoes Room, you'll find memorabilia from famous players. One is running back O. J. Simpson's jersey and helmet. He played for the Buffalo Bills and the San Francisco 49ers. His career record is 11,236 yards rushing, 203 receptions, and 990 yards on kickoff returns, for a combined net yardage of 14,368.

On display is the battered helmet of quarterback Y. A. Tittle. He played for the Baltimore Colts, the San Francisco 49ers, and the New York Giants. His career records were 2,427 completions, 33,070 yards, and 242 touchdowns.

Other souvenirs in the exhibit include halfback Earl "Dutch" Clark's Detroit Lions warm-up jacket. And, of course, you'll see jerseys from Roger Staubach and "Mean" Joe Greene. Staubach, the 1963 Heisman Trophy winner and quarterback for the Dallas Cowboys, helped the Cowboys win four NFC titles and two Super Bowls — numbers VI and XII. He was voted MVP in Super Bowl VI.

Defensive tackle Joe Greene was the number one draft pick of the Steelers in 1969. An exceptional team leader, he played in six AFC title games, ten **Pro Bowls**, and four Super Bowls.

Also in this building is the Super Bowl Series Room — a complete picture story of the championships, featuring stories and photos of each big game. Of particular note is a replica of the Vince Lombardi Trophy, given to the winning Super Bowl team, and replicas of the fabulous rings given to winning team members. For example, the rings from Super Bowl XVI have over two carats of diamonds, worth thousands of dollars.

Need a rest? Watch a video of Super Bowl highlights. Or go to the movies. Downstairs a theater shows a different NFL action film each hour.

The Black Man in Pro Football exhibit includes an interview with Fritz Pollard, a star halfback and the first black professional football coach.
Inset: O. J. Simpson, who played for the Buffalo Bills and the San Francisco 49ers, had a career record of 14,368 net yards.

300

VICTORIES . . . COACH DON SHULA

ON SEPTEMBER 22, 1991, DON SHULA RECORDED HIS 300TH
COACHING VICTORY WHEN HIS MIAMI DOLPHINS DEFEATED THE
GREEN BAY PACKERS, 16-13. ONLY ONE OTHER COACH, THE FABLED
GEORGE HALAS OF THE CHICAGO BEARS, RECORDED MORE
VICTORIES—325. HALAS' CAREER COVERED 40 YEARS WHILE
SHULA REACHED THE 300-WIN PLATEAU IN HIS 29TH SEASON. ON
DISPLAY HERE IS THE SHIRT SHULA WORE ON THE SIDELINE THE
DAY HE RECORDED HIS 300TH VICTORY.

AT THE TIME THAT SHULA REACHED THE 300-WIN MARK, HE HAD
A WINNING PERCENTAGE OF .681, WHICH IS THE BEST MARK
RECORDED BY ANY COACH WITH MORE THAN 17 SEASONS AND
122 VICTORIES. SEE THE RAILING DISPLAY FOR COMPLETE
RECORDS OF THE TOP TWENTY COACHES IN CAREER VICTORIES.

One exhibit commemorates the 300th victory posted by coach Don Shula when his
Miami Dolphins beat the Green Bay Packers on September 22, 1991. Coaches
must be retired before they can be named to the Pro Football Hall of Fame.

Throughout the Hall of Fame you can participate in the adventure of football. There are many video monitors, taped voice recordings, question and answer boards, and interactive computers just for visitors.

How do football players get elected into the Hall of Fame? Any fan may nominate any pro football coach, contributor, or player by writing to the Pro Football Hall of Fame. A coach must be retired, but a player must have been retired for at least five years.

The Board of Selectors, made up of media representatives from each pro football city, five at-large representatives, and a representative from the Pro Football Writers Association, elects new members. To make sure that older players are on the ballot, a Senior Committee of five veteran members nominates one person who played a majority of his career 25 years prior to the year of the class being considered.

The entire board meets every year, on the day before the Super Bowl game, to elect players. To be elected, a nominee needs 80 percent of the votes. Rules say that between four and seven people are to be elected each year.

In 1993 the board elected two coaches — Chuck Noll and Bill Walsh — and three players — Dan Fouts, Larry Little, and Walter Payton.

When Chuck Noll became coach for the Pittsburgh Steelers, the Steelers hadn't won a championship of any kind. Noll is the only coach to win four Super Bowls — IX, X, XIII, and XIV.

Bill Walsh, head coach for the San Francisco 49ers from 1979 to 1988, won three Super Bowls — XVI, XIX, and XXIII, in 1982, 1985, and 1989. When he took over the 49ers in 1979, the team had lost 14 games and won 2. Three years later, with Walsh's coaching, the 49ers went on to win the NFL Championship.

Dan Fouts, quarterback for the San Diego Chargers, established a record for the most 300-yard passing games, with 51, and played in six Pro Bowls. At the time of his election to the Hall of Fame, Fouts was only one of three quarterbacks to throw more than 40,000 yards in a career.

Larry Little played in 183 games for the San Diego Chargers and the Miami Dolphins from 1967 to 1980, the 1969 AFL All-Star game, four Pro Bowls, and three consecutive Super Bowls, 1971 to 1973. He was also an all-pro selection six times.

Walter Payton is the NFL's all-time leading rusher, with 16,726 yards and 110 rushing touchdowns. He played in nine Pro Bowls and holds the single game rushing record, with 275 yards against the Minnesota Vikings in 1977.

Every summer the Pro Football Hall of Fame hosts Football's Greatest Weekend. After a parade, the new members are inducted on the front steps of the Hall of Fame. Then the AFC-NFC Hall of Fame preseason football game is played at Fawcett Stadium, a high school arena that holds 22,000 fans.

Since its opening in September 1963, more than five million people — from the United States and over 60 foreign countries — have visited the Pro Football Hall of Fame and seen its mementoes. And each memento brings back the roar of the crowd and the thrill of the touchdown.

The Mementoes Room in the Pro Football Hall of Fame features such items as quarterback/placekicker George Blanda's shirt and the battered helmet of quarterback Y. A. Tittle.

Fullback Jim Brown played nine seasons with the Cleveland Browns and was inducted into the Pro Football Hall of Fame in 1971.

Pro Football
Hall of Fame Members

Canton, Ohio

Electees to the Hall of Fame

Adderley, Herb 1980
Alworth, Lance 1978
Atkins, Doug 1982
Badgro, Morris "Red" 1981
Barney, Lem 1992
*Battles, Cliff 1968
Baugh, Sammy 1963
Bednarik, Chuck 1967
*Bell, Bert 1963
Bell, Bobby 1983
Berry, Raymond 1973
*Bidwill, Charles W., Sr. 1967
Biletnikoff, Fred 1988
Blanda, George 1981
Blount, Mel 1989
Bradshaw, Terry 1989
Brown, Jim 1971
*Brown, Paul E. 1967
Brown, Roosevelt 1975
Brown, Willie 1984
*Buchanan, Buck 1990
Butkus, Dick 1979
Campbell, Earl 1991
Canadeo, Tony 1974
*Carr, Joe 1963
*Chamberlin, Guy 1965
*Christiansen, Jack 1970
*Clark, Earl "Dutch" 1963
Connor, George 1975
*Conzelman, Jimmy 1964
Csonka, Larry 1987
Davis, Al 1992
Davis, Willie 1981

Dawson, Len 1987
Ditka, Mike 1988
Donovan, Art 1968
*Driscoll, John "Paddy" 1965
Dudley, Bill 1966
Edwards, Albert Glen "Turk"
    1969
Ewbank, Weeb 1978
Fears, Tom 1970
Flaherty, Ray 1976
*Ford, Leonard "Len" 1976
Fortmann, Daniel J., M.D. 1965
Fouts, Dan 1993
Gatski, Frank 1985
*George, Bill 1974
Gifford, Frank 1977
Gillman, Sid 1983
Graham, Otto 1965
*Grange, Harold "Red" 1963
Greene, Joe 1987
Gregg, Forrest 1977
Griese, Bob 1990
Groza, Lou 1974
*Guyon, Joe 1966
*Halas, George 1963
Ham, Jack 1988
Hannah, John 1991
Harris, Franco 1990
*Healey, Ed 1964
*Hein, Mel 1963
Hendricks, Ted 1990
*Henry, Wilbur "Pete" 1963
*Herber, Arnie 1966

*Hewitt, Bill 1971
*Hinkle, Clarke 1964
Hirsch, Elroy "Crazy Legs" 1968
Hornung, Paul 1986
Houston, Ken 1986
*Hubbard, Robert "Cal" 1963
Huff, Sam 1982
Hunt, Lamar 1972
Hutson, Don 1963
Johnson, John Henry 1987
Jones, David "Deacon" 1980
Jones, Stan 1991
Jurgensen, Sonny 1983
*Kiesling, Walt 1966
*Kinard, Frank "Bruiser" 1971
*Lambeau, Earl "Curly" 1963
Lambert, Jack 1990
Landry, Tom 1990
Lane, Richard "Night Train" 1974
Langer, Jim 1987
Lanier, Willie 1986
Lary, Yale 1979
Lavelli, Dante 1975
*Layne, Bobby 1967
*Leemans, Alphonse "Tuffy" 1978
Lilly, Bob 1980
Little, Larry 1993
*Lombardi, Vince 1971
Luckman, Sid 1965
*Lyman, William Roy "Link" 1964
Mackey, John 1992
*Mara, Tim 1963

Marchetti, Gino 1972
*Marshall, George Preston 1963
Matson, Ollie 1972
Maynard, Don 1987
McAfee, George 1966
McCormack, Mike 1984
McElhenny, Hugh 1970
*McNally, John "Blood" 1963
Michalske, August "Mike" 1964
*Millner, Wayne 1968
Mitchell, Bobby 1983
Mix, Ron 1979
Moore, Leonard "Lenny" 1975
Motley, Marion 1968
Musso, George 1982
*Nagurski, Bronko 1963
Namath, Joe 1985
*Neale, Earle "Greasy" 1969
*Nevers, Ernie 1963
Nitschke, Ray 1978
Noll, Chuck 1993
Nomellini, Leo 1969
Olsen, Merlin 1982
Otto, Jim 1980
*Owen, Steven 1966
Page, Alan 1988
Parker, Clarence "Ace" 1972
Parker, Jim 1973
Payton, Walter 1993
Perry, Fletcher "Joe" 1969
Pihos, Pete 1970
*Ray, Hugh "Shorty" 1966
*Reeves, Dan 1967
Riggins, John 1992
Ringo, Jim 1981

Robustelli, Andy 1971
*Rooney, Art 1964
Rozelle, Pete 1985
St. Clair, Bob 1990
Sayers, Gale 1977
Schmidt, Joe 1973
Schramm, Tex 1991
Shell, Art 1989
Simpson, O. J. 1985
Starr, Bart 1977
Staubach, Roger 1985
Stautner, Ernie 1969
Stenerud, Jan 1991
*Strong, Ken 1967
*Stydahar, Joe 1967
Tarkenton, Fran 1986
Taylor, Charley 1984
Taylor, Jim 1976
*Thorpe, Jim 1963
Tittle, Y. A. 1971
*Trafton, George 1964
Trippi, Charley 1968
*Tunnell, Emlen 1967
Turner, Clyde "Bulldog" 1966
Unitas, Johnny 1979
Upshaw, Gene 1987
*Van Brocklin, Norm 1971
Van Buren, Steve 1965
Walker, Doak 1986
Walsh, Bill 1993
Warfield, Paul 1983
*Waterfield, Bob 1965
Weinmeister, Arnie 1984
Willis, Bill 1977
Wilson, Larry 1978

*Wojciechowicz, Alex 1968
Wood, Willie 1989

*Deceased

Glossary

barnstorming tour A tour in which a team travels around the country playing exhibition games during the off-season.

draft A process in which teams take turns selecting top players.

fumble A ball that slips out of a player's hands.

Pro Bowl A postseason NFL game that matches stars from the NFC against stars from the AFC.

promoter Someone who hopes to find profit by staging an athletic event for which tickets are sold.

punt To drop the ball and kick it before it reaches the ground.

rookie An athlete playing as a professional for the first time.

rugby A kind of football game named after a famous English public school.

scrimmage A practice game between players.

Super Bowl The yearly play-off game between the two conferences of the National Football League.

touchdown A goal scored when a team runs or passes the ball over the opponent's goal line.

In 1972, the Miami Dolphins played a perfect season with 17 wins and no losses. The team's accomplishment is marked in a Hall of Fame exhibit.

Index

Richard "Night Train" Lane, inducted into the Pro Football Hall of Fame in 1974, played as a cornerback for the Los Angeles Rams, the Chicago Cardinals, and the Detroit Lions.

DATE DUE

FE 27'96			
90. 02.기마			
			DEMCO 25-380